Dick and Fitzgerald

The Camp Fire Songster

A Collection of Popular, Patriotic, National, Pathetic and Jolly Songs

Dick and Fitzgerald

The Camp Fire Songster
A Collection of Popular, Patriotic, National, Pathetic and Jolly Songs

ISBN/EAN: 9783337255145

Printed in Europe, USA, Canada, Australia, Japan

Cover: Foto ©Andreas Hilbeck / pixelio.de

More available books at **www.hansebooks.com**

THE

CAMP-FIRE SONGSTER;

A COLLECTION OF

POPULAR, PATRIOTIC, NATIONAL, PATHETIC,
AND JOLLY SONGS,

SUITED FOR THE CAMP OR MARCH,

CONTAINING A NUMBER OF SONGS NEVER BEFORE PRINTED.

———————

NEW YORK:

DICK & FITZGERALD, PUBLISHERS.

CONTENTS.

THE CAMP-FIRE SONGSTER.

HOW ARE YOU, JOHNNY BULL?

Tune—"Whack ! Row de Dow."

Our Country is in danger against a foreign foe ;
Old England swears her bulls and bears to war are
      bound to go ;
Since '76 they've tried to fix a cause to raise a row ;
While rebellion's hot they think they've got a chance
      to whale us now.

      With a whack ! row de dow,
        How are *you*. Johnny Bull ?
      Whack ! row de dow,
        Oh ! Yankee Doodle doo.

Our glory ! it to us is dear, our Union's dearer still !
John Bull will find, if he goes it blind, of fight he'll get
      his fill.
But I have heard if a little word will save our
      Constitution,
We'll save that first, then dare the worst, ere yield to
      dissolution.

      With a whack ! row de dow,
        How are *you*. Johnny Bull ?
      Whack ! row de dow,
        Oh ! Yankee Doodle doo.

But, then, if England wants to fight, (this verse I'll sing
  you next,)
If she is bound to have a round, under some poor pre-
  text,
Then let her come! we'll send her home, as we did
  once before ;
We've licked her twice, just like a mice, and can do the
  same once more.

     With a whack! row de dow,
       How are *you*, Johnny Bull?
     Whack ! row de dow.
     Oh ! Yankee Doodle doo.

If such a fierce alternative is forced upon our land,
E'en Southern men will rally then, and think it time
  to stand !
Brothers may clash, in conflict rash. while quarreling's
  all our own ;
But if we unite, together fight, we'll shake old England's throne.

     With a whack ! row de dow,
       How are *you*, Johnny Bull?
     Whack! row de dow,
     Oh ! Yankee Doodle doo.

And Ireland, too, will rise and do what's been her hope
  for years ;
Strike at the *Lion* that crushed O'Brien, bedewed their
  soil with tears !
For they know that we sent breadstuffs, free, in their
  dark hour of trial ;
They'll arm and fight, stand by the right, in true old
  Irish style.

     With a whack ! row de dow,
       How are *you*, Johnny Bull?
     Whack ! row de dow,
     Oh ! Yankee Doodle doo.

And there's Lou Napoleon, he's got a bone to pick;
He may urge them on, and then come down, just like a
thousand of brick;
For he bears in mind how they confined his sire in St.
Helena—
I owe you one, when war's begun I'll give you philo-
pœna.

With a whack ! row de dow,
How are *you*, Johnny Bull?
Whack ! row de dow,
Oh ! Yankee Doodle doo.

The Southerns are in earnest, they'll whip us if they
can—
'Tis plain to see, to you or me, " or any other man ;"
Then let us swear we'll do or dare—the Union, hence;
so be it !
We *may* be whipt, our old Flag stript, but I, for one,
" don't see it !"

With a whack ! row de dow,
How are *you*, Johnny Bull?
Whack ! row de dow,
Oh ! Yankee Doodle doo.

We'll sing of brave McClellan, and glorious General
Scott ;
But there's a few, who are as true, that are remem-
bered not ;
'Tis the private bold, who, not for gold, goes where the
bullets rattle,
He may fight and die, unnoticed lie, upon the field of
battle.

With a whack ! row de dow,
How are *you*, Johnny Bull?
Whack ! row de dow,
Oh ! Yankee Doodle doo.

THERE LIES THE WHISKEY BOTTLE, EMPTY ON THE SHELF.

TUNE—"John Brown's Song."

Music published by Russel & Tolman, 291 Washington st., Boston.

McClellan is our leader now, we've had our last retreat;
McClellan is our leader now, we've had our last retreat;
McClellan is our leader now, we've had our last retreat;
    We'll now go marching on.

        Say, brothers, will you meet us?
        Say, brothers, will you meet us?
        Say, brothers, will you meet us?
          As we go marching on.

Thomas turned a *Somerset*, and gave the rebels rats;
Thomas turned a *Somerset*, and gave the rebels rats;
Thomas turned a *Somerset*, and gave the rebels rats;
    And sent them rolling home.

        Oh, brothers, we will join him;
        Oh, brothers, we will join him;
        Oh, brothers, we will join him;
          And send them rolling home.

How are you, Johnny Bull, old boy? How are you,
    Johnny Bull?
How are you, Johnny Bull, old boy? How are you,
    Johnny Bull?
If you want to fight, old Roast Beef, you will get your
    belly full,
    And then go rolling home.

        Oh, Johnny, don't you fight us;
        Oh, Johnny, don't you fight us;
        Oh, Johnny, don't you fight us;
          Or we'll send you rolling home.

We'll have a farm in Dixie, boys, and put some niggers
    on it ;
We'll have a farm in Dixie, boys, and put some niggers
    on it ;
We'll have a farm in Dixie, boys, and put some niggers
    on it ;
    And then we'll simmer down.

        Oh, sisters, come and join us ;
        Oh, sisters, come and join us ;
        Oh, sisters, come and join us ;
          Way down in Dixie's land.

Oh, boys, we'll sip our cobbler's then, and cloud our
    Meerschaum pipes ;
Oh, boys, we'll sip our cobbler's then, and cloud our
    Meerschaum pipes ;
Oh, boys, we'll sip our cobbler's then, and cloud our
    Meerschaum pipes ;
    Way down in Dixie's land.

        Oh, bummers, come and meet us ;
        Oh, bummers, come and meet us ;
        Oh, bummers, come and meet us ;
          Way down in Dixie's land.

There lies the whiskey bottle empty on the shelf ;
There lies the whiskey bottle empty on the shelf ;
There lies the whiskey bottle empty on the shelf ;
    But there's more in the demi-john.

        Oh, bummers, don't you leave us ;
        Oh, bummers, don't you leave us ;
        Oh, bummers, don't you leave us ;
          We'll soon go marching on.

The girls we left behind us, boys, our sweethearts at
    the North ;
The girls we left behind us, boys, our sweethearts at
    the North ;

The girls we left behind us, boys, our sweethearts at
    the North,
Smile on us as we march.

      Oh, sweethearts, don't forget us ;
      Oh, sweethearts, don't forget us ;
      Oh, sweethearts, don't forget us ;
        We'll soon come marching home.

ABRAHAM'S DAUGHTER.

As sung, with unbounded applause, by Dan Bryant, in the bur-
lesque of "The Raw Recruits," and published with his permission.
The music, with Piano-Forte accompanyment, published by Firth,
Pond & Co., 547 Broadway, New York.

      Some years ago, I s'pose you know,
        Johnny Bull sent 'missioners
      To North and South of America,
        For to separate this Union :
      He tried it hard, with all his might,
        But didn't we give him a warmer? oh, oh, oh!

CHORUS.—Whilst we're here, if they interfere,
        Won't we give them a warmer !
      Oh! I'm a going down to Washington,
        To fight for Abraham's daughter.

      Now, there's Napoleon, right from France,
        He swears he'll be revenged, oh !
      If Johnny Bull sends his farmyard
        To the Southern ports, oh !
      He'll rush right in and tear his skin,
        Killkenny is behind, oh, oh, oh !

        Whilst we're here, &c.

      Oh! Johnny Bull is gone to grass,
        To fatten up his calves, oh !
      He's talking of sending a shilling-a-day
        Soldiers to the South, oh !
      But we licked them well, in 1812,
        And we can whip them weller: oh, oh, oh !

        Whilst we're here, &c.

I LOVE A SIXPENCE.

I love a sixpence, jolly, jolly sixpence,
  I love a sixpence as I do my life ;
I'll save a penny of it, I'll spend a penny of it,
  I'll take fourpence of it home to my wife.

  For the pipe and the bowl shall greet us,
  Kind friends will ne'er deceive us,
  And happy is the man that shall meet us,
    As we go rolling home.
  Rolling home, rolling home, rolling home,
  Rolling home, rolling home, rolling home,
  And happy is the man that shall meet us,
    As we go rolling home.

I love a fivepence, jolly, jolly fivepence,
  I love a fivepence as I love my life ;
I'll save a penny of it, I'll spend a penny of it,
  I'll take threepence of it home to my wife.

  For the pipe and the bowl shall greet us, &c.

WHACK! ROW DE DOW.

Sung by Dan Bryant, at the hall of Bryant's Minstrels, 472 Broadway, N. Y., and published with his permission. The music published by Firth, Pond & Co., 547 Broadway, N. Y.

  Good people all, both great and small,
  Come listen to my song,
  If you've got a little time to spare,
  I won't detain you long ;
  'Tis of our Flag, our Nation's brag,
  Our Union and our Constitution,:
  For the Stars and Stripes must wave
  'Till the day of resurrection, with a

    Whack ! row de dow.
  The Stars and Stripes must wave forever,
      Whack ! row de dow :
  For our Flag we're bound to save.

Down South, there's General Beauregard,
With his rebel crew,
Who says he'll make us Northern folks,
Nip up dee doo den do ;
We'll have no more Bull-Run affairs,
Where the chivalry say we did knock under ;
For we've got a brave McClellan now,
Who will give them Northern thunder.

        Whack ! row de dow ;
How ARE you, General Bowgun ?
        Whack ! row de dow ;
Dat's wat's de matter.

Now, there's our gallant Sixty-ninth,
Who never flinch for trifles,
And our bully boys, the Fire Zouaves,
With their little Minié Rifles ;
And first of all in duty's call,
The Massachusetts boys so handy,
Who will show the Southern chivalry,
No fool is Yankee Doodle dandy.

        Whack ! row de dow ;
No fool is Yankee Doodle dandy;
        Whack ! row de dow,
Yankee Doodle doo.

In speaking of our Fire-Zouaves,
Reminds me of a fact :
They've proved they don't do things by halves,
Nor take the backward track.
At the Battle of Bull Run,
They fought their way so bravely ;
Oh ! they did lay low to trap the foe—
How are ye, Black Horse cavalry ?

        Whack ! row de dow ;
The boys, they were on hand, I tell you.
        Whack ! row de dow ;
Oh ! Syksey, take de but.

FREE AND EASY STILL.

AIR—Gay and Happy.

Published with the permission of Henry McCaffrey, Baltimore,
owner of the copyright, and publisher of the words and music.

I'm the lad that's free and easy,
Wheresoe'er I chance to be ;
And I'll do my best to please ye,
If you will but list to me.

CHORUS.—So let the world jog along as it will,
I'll be free and easy still.

Some there are who meet their troubles,
Others drown their cares in drink ;
All our trials are but bubbles—
Fretting forges many a link.
So let the world, &c.

I envy neither great nor wealthy,
Poverty I ne'er despise ;
Let me be contented, healthy,
And the boon I'll dearly prize.
So let the world, &c.

The great have cares I little know of—
All that glitters is not gold ;
Merit's seldom made a show of,
And true worth is rarely told.
So let the world, &c.

Why, then, waste our time in fretting—
The longest lane must have an end,
Industry strives hard in getting
Stores for fools and knaves to spend.
So let the world, &c,

I care for all, yet care for no man—
Those who mean well should not fear ;
I like a man, and love a woman—
What else makes this life so dear ?
So let the world, &c.

GAY AND HAPPY.

Published with the permission of Henry McCaffrey, Baltimore, owner of the copyright, and publisher of the words and music.

I am the girl that's gay and happy,
   And I your attention call ;
If you'll listen to my story,
   I will try to please you all.

CHORUS.—So let the world jog along as it will,
   I'll be gay and happy still ;
   Gay and happy, gay and happy,
   I'll be gay and happy still.

If the President sat beside me,
   I would sing with usual glee ;
He might smile or frown upon me,
   Still I'd sing and happy be.

   So let the world, &c.

If a man be poor and needy,
   I could never pass him by ;
' But with kindness I would treat him.
   And this world I would enjoy.

   So let the world, &c.

You may say : the rich and wealthy
   Poverty they do despise,
I am content, tho' poor, but healthy :
   Health is the only boon I prize.

   So let the world &c.

In the South they threaten disunion,
   If the North will not obey ;
But the spirit of General Washington
   Still keeps guard with Henry Clay.

   So let the world, &c.

Here's success to Major Anderson,
   The hero, and his gallant band,
Ever ready to protect, or die
   To save his native land.

     So let the world, &c.

With our hands and hearts united,
   With the Constitution stand ;
The Union and our Flag for ever,
   The Stars and Stripes, and our native land.

    So let the world, &c.

Now, my friends, my song is ended,
   Let the world wag as it will ;
Every night I'll try to please you,
   I'll be gay and happy still.

     So let the world, &c.

BULLY FOR US.

A little song I'm going to sing,
   Bully for us, bully for us,
To please you all I'll do the thing,
   Bully for me, bully for me ;
Some things now are very fine,
   So dey are, so dey are,
I'll sing a verse or two in rhyme,
   Bully for us, bully for us.

CHORUS—Bully, O bully, O bully for us,
     Bully for us, bully for us,
  Join in the chorus and hab some fun,
    Bully for us, bully for us.

Major Anderson is a brave man,
 Dat's a fact, dat's a fact,
He's de man to fight for our land,
 Bully for him, bully for him;
We will give him a helping hand,
 So we will, so we will,
Three cheers for him and his little band,
 Hip hurrah, hip hurrah.

  Bully, O bully, &c,

Of generals now we have a lot,
 So we have, so we have,
The first of all is General Scott,
 Bully for him, bully for him ;
And to his country he's always true,
 Dat's a fact, dat's a fact ;
He stands by de Red, White and Blue,
 Bully for us, bully for us.

  Bully, O bully, &c.

Abe Lincoln now is in de chair,
 So he is, so he is,
But wont he make some folks stare?
 I'll bet he will, I'll bet he will ;
By de Union now he's bound to stand,
 I believe you, I believe you,
With Bill Seward on his right hand,
 Bully for them, bully for them.

  Bully, O bully, &c.

Now, my song I'll bring to an end,
 I think it's time, I think it's time,
I hope no one it did offend,
 Dat's a fact, dat's a fact ;
De Union now must be preserved,
 So it must, so it must,
And treat traitors as they deserve,
 Hang them up, hang them up.

  Bully, O bully, &c.

From Donelson old Floyd he stole,
    Bully old thief, bully old thief,
And like a rat went into his hole,
    Bully for us, bully for us.
The rebels from Manassas ran,
    So they did, so they did,
But we will catch them if we can,
    Bully for us, bully for us.

    Bully, O bully, &c.

JEFF DAVIS;

OR,

THE KING OF THE SOUTHERN DOMINIONS.

Air—The King of the Cannibal Islands.

Come, listen now, and you will hear
    About a joke that's very queer—
I have it in my mind quite clear:
    The King of the Southern Dominions,
His Court he did at Richmond fix,
And built his palace of stolen bricks;
On Sumter fort he played his tricks,
    And with big balls " put in big licks,"
And his name was Jeff, and to him clang
A rebel, traitorous, thieving gang,
And Uncle Sam swore soon he would hang
    This King of the Southern Dominions,
And rebel crew, so high and dry
That to come down in vain they'd try,
And then would be " all in my eye,"
    The King of the Southern Dominions.

On Washington his longing eyes,
    He turned, resolved to seize the prize,
And there would feast and gormandize
    The King of the Southern Dominions;

His aids, Slidel and the gay Yancey,
With Floyd, who robb'd the Treasury,
Wigfall, renowned for his bravery,
And Twiggs who is skilled in knavery,
And others of a cast the same,
To work the plot determined came ;
But Uncle Sam had bluffed their game—
    And the King of the Southern Dominions' ;
For soon with trumpet, fife and drum,
Marched his armies, and they were "some,"
And they "played out" 'tis true, by gum,
    The King of the Southern Dominions.

HAPPY LAND OF CANAAN.

You may talk about de times,
    But jes listen to my rhymes :
It brings to you de news accordin',
    It tells you how to catch
Old Jeff and Beauregard,
    And fotch 'em to de happy land of Canaan.

CHORUS.—Oh ! oh ! oh ! æ ! æ ! æ ! ah !
    De people in de South am getting mighty hot ;
    But afore dey know, old Jeff will get a shot
    Dat will send him to the happy land of Canaan.

Oh ! the rebels, they can blow,
    As all ob you may know,
Kase dey beat us at de battle of Bull-Run ;
    But when we come on dem again,
We shall show dem some fun,
    And bring dem to de happy land of Canaan.
            Oh, oh, oh ! &c.

Oh ! white folks, I s'pose you read
    'Bout old Jeff and his white steed,
Dat was seen in dat engagement ;
    Says a Union Volunteer,
Oh ! I'd like to pop him dere,
    And squash him to de happy land of Canaan.
            Oh, oh, oh ! &c.

Oh! de Fire Zouaves were dere,
    Dey made de Black-Horse cavalry stare ;
De way dey fought on dat occasion,
    Dey made dem open deir eyes,
And look in great surprise,
And wish dey were in de happy land of Canaan.

     Oh, oh, oh ! &c.

THE UNION.

Air—Root Hog or Die.

Away down in South Carolina they're kicking up a
    muss ;
By bombarding Fort Sumter they surely make it worse ;
They cannot split the Union, I'll tell you the reason
    why:
The Newburg boys will make them sing : Root hog or
    die.

The Seceshers at Baltimore, not many months ago,
They tried to rule the city, as you very well do know ;
They could not come the game, sir, I will tell you the
    reason why :
The Union boys will make them sing : Root hog or die.

The Plug Uglies they did muster, and tried to run us
    out,
But we had some Union hard stuff that made them look
    about ;
They could not make us leave the place, I'll tell you
    the reason why :
The Union boys made them sing : Root hog or die.

It was early in the day, boys, at the sound of drum and
    fife,
We marched away from home, so full of youth and life;
We are bound to gain the day, I'll tell you the reason
    why :
The Union boys will make them sing : Root hog or die.

As for Jeff Davis, we will put him back apace,
We will whip his Southern traitors with the very best
    of grace ;
They will not stand or make a show, I'll tell you the
    reason why :
The Union boys will make them sing : Root hog or die.

The Black Horse cavalry was becoming all the rage,
But the New York Zouaves caught them, and put them
    in a cage ;
With Ellsworth at their head, the rebels they did defy,
The Southern traitors had to sing : Root hog or die.

So rally around our colors, boys, and rush into the
    fray ;
And when the wars are over, we will sing another lay.
Here's to the Union and the Constitution ! we all join
    in the cry :
The Union, boys, for evermore : Root hog or die.

MY LOVE HE IS A ZOU-ZU.

My love he is a Zou-zu, so gallant and bold,
He's rough and he's handsome, scarce nineteen years
    old ;
To show off in Washington, he has left his own dear,
And my heart is a breaking because he's not here.

CHORUS.—For his spirit was brave : it was fierce to be-
    hold,
In a young man breed a Zou-zu, only nineteen years
    old.

His parents taught him to be a cavalier,
But the life of a Zou-zu he much did prefer ;
For his heart's with his Country in right or in wrong,
And in Richmond with Lozier he'll be afore long.

               For his spirit, &c.

My fond heart is beating for him constantly,
But I fear his affections may waver from me ;
For a sweetheart can be found in each State I am told,
By a young man, a Zou-zu, only nineteen years old.

For his spirit, &c.

And now for my Zou-zu I grieve and repine,
For fear that his brave heart may never be mine ;
All the wealth of Jeff Davis in cotton or gold,
I would give for my Zou-zu, only nineteen years old.

For his spirit, &c.

VIVA L' AMERICA.

Published by permission of FIRTH, POND & Co., 547 Broadway,
N. Y., owners of the copyright, and publishers of the words and
music.

Noble Republic ! happiest of lands,
Foremost of nations, Columbia stands ;
Freedom's proud banner floats in the skies,
Where shouts of Liberty daily arise.
"United we stand, divided we fall,"
Union forever, freedom to all.

CHORUS.—Throughout the world our motto shall be,
Viva l'America, home of the free.

Should ever traitor rise in the land,
Curs'd be his homestead, wither'd his hand ;
Shame be his mem'ry, scorn be his lot,
Exile his heritage, his name a blot !
"United we stand, divided we fall,"
Granting a home and freedom to all.

Throughout the world, &c.

To all her heroes, justice and fame,
To all her foes, a traitors foul name ;   [wave,
Our "Stripes and Stars" still proudly shall
Emblem of Liberty, flag of the brave.
"United we stand, divided we fall,"
Gladly we'll die at our country's call.

Throughout the world, &c.

OUR FLAG IS THERE.

Our Flag is there ! our Flag is there !
  We'll hail it with three loud huzzas ;
Our Flag is there ! our Flag is there !
  Behold the glorious Stripes and Stars !
Stout hearts have fought for that bright Flag,
  Strong hands sustained it mast-head high,
And, oh ! to see how proud it waves,
  Brings tears of joy in every eye.

CHORUS.—Our Flag is there ! our Flag is there !
      We hail it with three loud huzzas ;
      Our Flag is there ! our Flag is there !
      Behold the glorious Stripes and Stars !

That Flag has stood the battle's roar,
  With foemen stout, with foemen brave ;
Strong hands have strove that Flag to lower,
  And found a speedy watery grave !
That flag is known on every shore,
  The standard of a gallant band,
Alike sustained in peace or war,
  It floats o'er Freedom's happy land.

Our Flag is there, &c.

THE UNION MUST AND SHALL BE PRESERVED.

AIR—Star Spangled Banner.

Oh ! say, can a thought so vile and base come
  To the mind of a dweller on Columbia's soil,
That the work of our fathers should now be undone,
  And unwound should now be the proud national
    coil?
And that traitors should sway and rule o'er this proud
    land,
With tyranny's lash, and the plunderer's brand !
No, never ! Freemen, never ! With the right, our arm
    nerved,
The Union it must and shall be preserved.

And though traitor may spring from 'mong kindred
    and friends,
  Let them look to themselves, to the Union we're
    true ;
If their hearts will prove false let its blood make
    amends,
  And the stain we'll wash off while our hands we
    imbue !
Neither love of friends false or kindred shall save
Them the terror of flight, and the gloom of the
    grave ;
Let them look to themselves, with the right our arm
    nerved,
The Union it must and shall be preserved !

If a son or a father prove false to the flag,
  Then sever the tie with which nature has bound you,
And remember, though anguish your own heart may
    drag
  To despair, that the love of your country has found
    you.

And, whatever the issue be of this foul strife,
Be sure that it cost not fair Liberty's life.
Then let traitors beware ! with the right our arm nerved,
The Union it must and shall be preserved !

Oh ! thus be it ever when freemen shall stand
    Between their loved homes and fraternal blood spill-
       ing ;
May they ever be guided, great God, by thy hand,
    To obey thy just laws and commandments be willing,
And a prosperous nation we ever shall be,
With true love for our Country and full trust in Thee.
Grant these blessings, Jehovah ! with the right still us
       nerve,
While the Union we rush to uphold and preserve !

ANNIE LAURIE.

Maxwelton Braes are bonnie,
Where early fa's the dew,
And it's there that Annie Laurie
Gie'd me her promise true ;
Gie'd me her promise true,
Which ne'er forget will be,
And for bonnie Annie Laurie
I'd lay me doune and dee.

Her brow is like the snaw-drift,
Her throat is like the swan ;
Her face it is the fairest
That e'er the sun shone on,
That e'er the sun shone on,
And dark blue is her e'e ;
And for bonnie Annie Laurie
I'd lay me doune and dee.

Like dew on the gowan lying,
Is the fa' o' her fairy feet,
And like the winds in Summer sighing,
Her voice is low and sweet,

Her voice is low and sweet,
And she's a' the world to me ;
And for bonnie Annie Laurie
I'd lay me doune and dee.

THE NEW YORK VOLUNTEER.

'Twas in the days of '76,
  When Freemen, young and old,
All fought for Independence then,
  Each hero brave and bold !
'Twas then the noble Stars and Stripes
  In triumph did appear,
And defended by brave patriots,
  The Yankee Volunteers.

CHORUS.—'Tis my delight to march and fight .
  Like a New York Volunteer.

Now, there's our City Regiments,
  Just see what they have done :
The first to offer to the State
  To go to Washington
To protect the Federal Capital
  And the Flag they love so dear !
And they've done their duty nobly,
  Like New York Volunteers.

    'Tis my delight, &c.

The Rebels out in Maryland,
  They madly raved, and swore
They'd let none of our Union troops
  Pass through Baltimore ;
But the Massachusetts Regiment
  No Traitors did they fear ;
But fought their way to Washington,
  Like Yankee Volunteers.

    'Tis my delight, &c.

Now, there's the noble Sixty-Ninth,
    Just see what they have done :
They dug ten miles of trenches,
    Way down at Washington.
Now, they are reorganizing
    Under Thomas Francis Meagher,
And they'll avenge brave Corcoran,
    Like New York Volunteers.

'Tis my delight, &c,

Then, there's the noble Firemen,
    Ever ready, one and all,
To quench the burning elements,
    And obey their Country's call ;
They never shrink from duty,
    But you'll always find them near,
To avenge brave Col. Ellsworth
    Like New York Volunteers.

'Tis my delight, &c.

VIVE LA COMPAGNIE.

Let Bacchus' to Venus libations pour forth,
    Vive la compagnie !
And let us make use of our time while it lasts,
    Vive la compagnie !

CHORUS :—Oh ! vive la, vive la, vive l'amour,
    Vive la, vive la, vive l'amour,
    Vive l'amour, vive l'amour,
    Vive la compagnie !

Let every old bachelor fill up his glass,
    Vive la compagnie !
And drink to the health of his favorite lass,
    Vive l'compagnie !

Oh ! Vive la, &c.

Let every married man drink to his wife,
        Vive la compagnie !
The friend of his bosom and comfort of life,
        Vive la compagnie !

    Oh ! vive la, &c.

Come, fill up your glasses—I'll give you a toast,
        Vive la compagnie !
Here's a health to our friend—our kind, worthy host,
        Vive la compagnie !

    Oh ! vive la, &c.

Since all, with good humor, I've toasted so free,
        Vive la compagnie !
I hope it will please you to drink now with me,
        Vive la compagnie !

    Oh ! vive la, &c.

———

BENNY HAVENS.

Come, fill your glasses, fellows, and stand up in a row,
To sentimental drinking we are going for to go ;
In the army there's sobriety—promotion very slow,
So we'll sigh o'er reminiscenses of Benny Havens, O !

CHORUS.—Benny Havens, O ! Benny Havens,
We'll sigh o'er reminiscences of Benny Havens,

Let us toast our foster father, the Republic, as you know,
Who in the path of science taught us upward for to grow,
And then the ladies of our land, whose cheeks like roses
    glow,
Who were oft remembered in our cups at Benny Havens, O!

    Benny Havens, &c.

To the ladies of America, whose hearts and albums, too,
Bear sad remembrance of the wrongs that stripling
    soldiers do,
We bid a long farewell, the best recompense we know,
Our loves and rhymings had their source at Benny
    Havens, O !

        Benny Havens, &c.

Of the smile-wreathed maids, with virgin lips, like roses
    steeped in dew.
Who are to be our better halves, we'd like to take a
    view ;
But sufficient for the bridal day's the ill of it, you know,
So we'll cheer our hearts with chorusing old Benny
    Havens, O !

        Benny Havens, &c.

To the ladies of the army our cups shall overflow,
Companions of our exile, and a shield 'gainst every foe,
May they see their husbands Generals, with double pay,
    also,
And join us in our choruses of Benny Havens, O !

        Benny Havens, &c,

To our regiments now, fellows, we all must shortly go,
And look as grave as parsons when they speak of things
    below ;
We must cultivate the graces, do everything just so,
And never speak to ears polite of Benny Havens, O !

        Benny Havens, &c.

Here's a health to Gen'l Scott—God bless the old
    hero,
He's an honor to his country, and a terror to each foe—
May he long rest on his laurels, and sorrow never
    know—
May he live to see a thousand years, and Benny Havens, O!

        Benny Havens, &c.

Here's a health to General Taylor, whose rough and
    ready blow
Brought terror to the rancheros of braggart Mexico ;
May his country ne'er forget his deeds, and never fail
    to show
She holds him worthy of a place at Benny Havens, O !

      Benny Havens, &c..

When you and I, and Benny, and brave McClellan, too,
Are brought before the final board, our course of life to
    view,
May we never "fess" on any point, but then be told
    to go
To join the army of the blest, and Benny Havens, O !

      Benny Havens, &c.

May the army be augmented, promotion be less slow,
May our country in the time of peace be ready for the
    foe ;
May we find a soldier's resting-place beneath a soldier's
    blow,
And space enough beside our grave for Benny Havens, O !

      Benny Havens, &c.

To our comrades who have fallen, a cup before we go,
They poured their life-blood freely out, *pro-bono-publico ;*
No marble points the stranger to where they rest below,
They sleep neglected, far away from Benny Havens, O !

      Benny Havens, &c.

From the courts of death, and danger from Tampa's
    deadly shore,
Goes up the voice of manly grief : O'Brien is no more !
In the land of sun and flowers his head lies buried low,
No more to sing "Petite Coquille," and Benny Havens, O !

      Benny Havens, &c.

THE FLAG OF OUR UNION.

BY GEN. GEO. P. MORRIS.

" A song for our banner ! "--the watchword recall
  Which gave the Republic a station :
" United we stand--divided we fall ! "
  It made and preserves us a nation !

CHORUS.--The union of lakes, the union of lands,
    The union of States none can sever ;
   The union of hearts, the union of hands,
    And the Flag of the Union forever and ever !
  The Flag of the Union forever !

What God in his mercy and wisdom design'd
  And arm'd with his weapons of thunder,
Not all the earth's despots and factions combined
  Have the power to conquer or sunder !

    The union of lakes, etc.

Oh ! keep the flag flying--the pride of the van,
  To all other nations display it !
The ladies for union are all to a—*man !*
  But not to the man who'd betray it.

    The union of lakes, etc.

THE GIRL I LEFT BEHIND ME.

The hour was sad I left the maid, a ling'ring farewell
  taking,
Her sighs and tears my steps delay'd, I thought her
  heart was breaking ;
In hurried words her name I bless'd, I breath'd the
  vows that bind me,
And to my heart in anguish press'd the girl I left behind me.

Then to the South we bore away, to win a name in story,
And there where dawns the sun of day, there dawn'd
 our sun of glory ;
Both blaz'd in noon on Freedom's height, where in the
 post assign'd me,
I shar'd the glory of that fight, sweet girl I left behind me.

Full many a name our banners bore, of former deeds of
 daring,
But they were days of Seventy-six, in which we had no
 sharing ;
But now *our* laurels freshly won, with the old ones shall
 entwin'd be,
Still worthy of our sires each son, sweet girl I left
 behind me.

The hope of final victory within my bosom burning,
Is mingling with sweet thoughts of thee, and of my
 fond returning ;
But should I ne'er return again, still worth thy love
 thou'lt find me,
Dishonor's breath shall never stain the name I'll leave
 behind me.

OUR COUNTRY'S FLAG.

AIR—Gay and Happy.

" Our Flag and the Union," in the North is the cry ;
" Our Flag and the Union," and for it we'll die ;
We'll let the South know the North don't lag
For plenty to defend our Country's bright flag !

CHORUS.—Then let the Southerners talk as they will,
 We'll fight for our Flag and the Union still ;
 Our Flag and the Union, our Flag and the Union,
 We'll fight for our Flag and the Union still.

Our Flag it shall wave o'er the land and the sea,
And the sons of the brave shall be happy and free ;
We'll be happy and free while our Flag shall fly,
And by its bright stars we will conquer or die !
 Then let the Southerners, &c.

In memory of our fathers who are under the sod,
We'll have but one Union, one Flag, and one God ;
And our Flag it shall be just the same as of old,
That was borne by the free and upheld by the bold.

    Then let the Southerners, &c.

Then our Union forever ! success to our tars,
And all brave defenders of the Stripes and Stars ;
When our flag is before us, borne by hearts brave and
    true,
Success is sure to follow with the Red, White and Blue.

    Then let the Southerners, &c.

HOME AGAIN.

Home again, home again,
  From a foreign shore,
And oh ! it fills my soul with joy
  To meet my friends once more.
Here I dropp'd the parting tear,
  To cross the ocean's foam,
But now I'm once again with those
  Who kindly greet me home.

Happy hearts, happy hearts,
  With mine have laughed in glee,
But, oh ! the friends I loved in youth,
  Seem happier to me.
And if my guide should be the fate,
Which bids me longer roam,
  But death alone can break the tie
That binds my heart to home.

Music sweet, music soft,
  Lingers round the place,
And oh ! I feel the childhood charm,
  That time cannot efface ;
Then give me but my homestead roof,
  I'll ask no palace dome,
For I can live a happy life
  With those I love at home.

OUR GERMAN VOLUNTEERS.

Air—New York Volunteers.

There is a General in the West whose deeds have come
    to fame,
He is a gallant soldier, and in movements he is game ;
Then let us raise our voices high and give three hearty
    cheers
For Siegal, hero of the West, and his German volun-
    teers :
For Siegel, hero of the West, and his German volun-
    teers.

Now, at the battle of Bull Run, we fought well, every
    one can say,
But panic struck our army, and we had to move away ;
And in that great confusion, of our rear we had great fears,
But it was protected by Blenker and his German volun-
    teers :
But it was protected by Blenker and his German volun-
    teers.

Now, there's the gallant Fifth Regiment who before
    their duty done,
They have again offered their services to go to Wash-
    ington ;
And were it not for Patterson, who did Scott's plan be-
    tray,
They would join McDowell at Bull Run, and took an
    active part that day :
They would join McDowell at Bull Run, and took an
    active part that day.

Then there's the gallant Max Weber, who took an ac-
    tive part,
When our ships of war bombarded Forts Hatteras and
    Clark ;
And should the South make an attack, while he and his
    men are there,
They'll get a mighty good whipping of which they are
    not aware :
They'll get a mighty good whipping of which they are
    not aware.

Now, as I close my little song, I'll say a word or two:
Should you be called upon to fight, stand by your
    colors true ;
Then raise your voices with one accord, and give three
    hearty cheers
For McClellan, Scott and Siegel, and their Union Vol-
    unteers !
For McClellan, Scott and Siegel, and their Union Vol-
    unteers !

THE UNION MARSEILLAISE.

Air—Marseillaise Hymn.

Arouse, ye men who love your Nation !
    Your starry standard boldly raise !
Disunion threats war's desolation,
    And Faction lights her dreadful blaze !
Oh ! shall we tamely list to treason,
    And hear our glorious land descried—
    Her laws, her charter, all defied
By traitors void of truth or reason ?
        Arise, Americans !
        The UNION ! 'tis your own !
March on ! march on ! all hearts as one !
    " REMEMBER WASHINGTON !"

By hatred nerved to deeds of daring,
    Our frantic foemen threatening stand,
No sacred tie nor memory sparing,
    Their madness spurns their native land !
Above our country's bosom glancing,
    Behold Disunion's murderous knife !
    Behold ! how rebels dare the strife,
In Slavery's horrid name advancing.
        Arise, American's !
        The UNION ! 'tis your own !
March on ! march on ! all hearts as one !
    " REMEMBER WASHINGTON !

Behold! how traitor tongues, misleading,
  Have fired the South with frantic rage;
Whilst demagogues, dissensions breeding,
  Have cast abroad war's bloody gage!
And shall we see our Union riven,
  Our martyrs' sacred graves defiled—
  Our patriot fathers' names reviled?
Arise, and answer—No! by Heaven!
    Arise, Americans!
    The UNION! 'tis your own!
March on! march on! all hearts as one!
  " REMEMBER WASHINGTON!

RED WHITE AND BLUE.

Oh! Columbia, the gem of the ocean,
  The home of the brave and the free,
The shrine of each patriot's devotion
  A world offers homage to thee!
Thy mandates make heroes assemble,
  When Liberty's form stands in view,
Thy banners make tyranny tremble,
  When borne by the Red, White and Blue.

CHORUS.--When borne by the Red, White and Blue!
    When borne by the Red, White and Blue!
    Thy banners make tyranny tremble,
    When borne by the Red, White and Blue.

When war raged it's wide desolation,
  And threaten'd our land to deform,
The ark then of freedom's foundation,
  Columbia, rode safe through the storm;
With her garland of victory o'er her,
  When so proudly she bore her bold crew,
With her flag proudly floating before her,
  The boast of the Red, White and Blue.

    The boast of, &c.

The wine cup, the wine cup bring hither,
   And fill you it up to the brim;
May the wreath they have won never wither,
   Nor the star of their glory grow dim;
May the service united ne'er sever,
   But hold to their colors so true,
The army and navy forever!
   Three cheers for the Red, White and Blue.

Three cheers, &c.

HURRAH FOR THE UNION.

AIR—Wait for the Wagon.

Come, brothers, all unite with us, come join us one and
   all,
United we must conquer, but divided we shall fall;
Our flag is for the Union, and we have a gallant crew,
Who have raised it, and who love it—'tis the Red,
   White and Blue.

CHORUS.—Then, hurrah for the Union! hurrah for the
     Union!
     Hurrah for the Union! and the Red, White
     and Blue!

Our ship's the Constitution, and good patriots at the
   helm
Will bring us into action, and our foes we'll over-
   whelm;
They'll find that we'll be wide awake enough to put
   them through—
Let our watchword be "The Union," and the Red,
   White and Blue.

Then, hurrah for the Union, &c.

Our flag shall be respected—not trampled in the dust—
The Stars and Stripes shall not come down, though
   traitors say they must;

Thank God, we have a captain, to his country ever
    true ;
We'll stand by Winfield Scott, and the Red, White and
    Blue.
        Then, hurrah for the Union, &c.

Come, then, all good and true men, and let us all unite,
With such a gallant leader we are sure to win the fight ;
Political distinctions late to the winds we threw ;
We fight but for the Union, and the Red, White and
    Blue.
        Then, hurrah for the Union, &c.

We fight to save the Union, and God is on our side ;
We fight to put down traitors who the Union would
    divide ;
And millions rally round our flag, which no power can
    subdue;
We can die—but we cannot pull down the Red, White
    and Blue.
        Then, hurrah for the Union, &c.

HOME, SWEET HOME.

'Mid pleasures and palaces though we may roam,
Be it ever so humble, there's no place like home ;
A charm from the skies seem to hallow us there,
Which, seek through the world, is ne'er met with else-
    where.

Chorus.—Home, home, sweet, sweet home,
        Be it ever so humble, there's no place like
        home.

An exile from home, splendor dazzles in vain ;
Oh ! give me my lowly thatched cottage again ;
The birds singing gayly that came at my call ;
Oh ! give me sweet peace of mind, dearer than all.

        Home, home, &c.

JONATHAN TO JOHN.

Air—John Anderson my Jo.

It don't seem hardly right, John,
　When both my hands was full,
To stump me to a fight, John—
　Your cousin, tu, John Bull!
　　　Ole Uncle S. sez he: "I guess
　　　We know it now," sez he:
　　　"The lion's paw is all the law,
　　　According to J. B."

Blood aint so cool as ink, John:
　It's likely you'd ha' wrote,
An' stopped a spell to think, John,
　Arter they' cut your throat?
　　　Ole Uncle S. sez he: "I guess
　　　He' skurce ha' stopped," sez he:
　　　"To mind his p's an' q's, ef that weazin'
　　　Hed belonged to ole J. B."

Who made the law that hurts, John.
　Heads I win—ditto tails?
"J. B." was on his shirts, John,
　Onless my memory fails.
　　　Uncle S. sez he: "I guess
　　　(I'm good at thet)," sez he:
　　　"Thet sauce for goose ain't jest the juice
　　　For ganders with J. B."

When your rights was our wrongs, John,
　You didn't stop for fuss—
Britanny's trident-prongs, John,
　Was good 'nough law for us.
　　　Ole Uncle S. sez he: "I guess
　　　Though physic's good," sez he:
　　　"It doesn't foller that he can swaller
　　　Prescriptions signed 'J. B.'"

Why talk so dreffle big, John,
  Of honor, when you meant
You didn't care a fig, John,
  But jest for *ten per cent*.
      Ole Uncle S. sez he: "I guess
      He's like the rest," sez he:
    "When all is done, it's number one
      That's nearest to J. B."

We give the critters back, John,   .
  Coz Abram thought 'twas right;
It warn't your bullyin' clack, John,
  Provokin' us to fight.
      Ole Uncle S. sez he: "I guess
      We've a hard row," sez he:
    "To hoe just now; but that, some how,
      May happen to J. B."

We ain't so weak an' poor, John,
  With twenty million people,
An' close to every door, John,
  A school house an' a steeple.
      Ole Uncle S. sez he: "I guess
      It is a fact," sez he:
    "The surest plan to make a man
      Is, think him so, J. B."

God means to make this land, John,
  Clear thru, from sea to sea,
Believe an' understand, John,
  The *wuth* o' bein free.
      Ole Uncle S. sez he: "I guess
      God's price is high," sez he: .
    "But nothin' else than wut he sells
      Wears long, an' thet, J. B."

THE CAMP WAR SONG.

Raise the Banner, raise it high, boys!
  Let it float against the sky;
" God be with us!" this our cry, boys;
  Under it we'll do, or die.

1st Cho.—Arise to glory, glory, glory!
      Our country calls—march on! march on!

2d Cho.—Co-ca-che-lunk-che-lunk-che-la-ly,
      Co-ca-che-lunk-che-lunk-che-lay,
      Co-ca-che-lunk-che-lunk-che-la-ly,
      Rig-a-ge-dig, and away we go!

Rebel miscreants, stand from under;
  Ye who bear the traitor's name!
Every star's a bolt of thunder—
  Every stripe a living flame!
        Arise, &c.

By our patriot sires in glory,
  By our sainted Washington,
We will fight, till every Tory
  Falls, that breathes beneath the sun!
        Arise, &c.

By our homes, our hearths, and altars,
  By our sweethearts, children, wives,
He who from our Union falters,
  Dies, hath he a thousand lives!
        Arise, &c.

Under Scott, our valiant leader,
  We will lay the traitors low;
Crushed to earth, each vile seceder
  Soon shall to our vengeance bow.
        Arise, &c.

Anderson! thy name shall cheer us
  'Mid the war field's bloody strife;
Old Fort Sumter yet shall hear us
  Call her battlements to life!
        Arise, &c.

God of battles! we implore Thee,
  Nerve our souls, make strong our arms ;
Bless us, as we bow before Thee,
  In the midst of war's alarms.

    Arise, &c.

Our spangled banner waving o'er us,
  We come, avengers of the free !
Shout, boys, shout ! the foe's before us !
  Union—God—and Liberty !

    Arise, &c

LITTLE RHODE ISLAND.
AIR—Nice little, tight little Island.

Of all the true host that New England can boast,
  From down by the sea unto highland,
No State is more true, or more willing to do,
  Than dear little Yankee Rhode Island.
    Loyal and true little Rhody !
    Bully for you, little Rhody !
Governor Sprague was not very vague,
When he said, " Shoulder arms ! Little Rhody !"

Not backward at all at the President's call,
  Nor yet with the air of a toady,
The gay little State, not a moment too late,
  Sent soldiers to answer for Rhody.
    Loyal and true little Rhody !
    Bully for you, little Rhody !
Governor Sprague was not very vague,
When he said, " Shoulder arms ! little Rhody !"

Two regiments raised, and by ev'ry one praised,
  Were soon on the march for head-quarters ;
All furnished first-rate at the cost of their State,
  And regular fighting dread-naughters !
    Loyal and true little Rhody !
    Bully for you, little Rhody !
Governor Sprague was not very vague,
When he said, " Shoulder arms ! little Rhody !"

Let traitors look out, for there's never a doubt
That Uncle Abe's army will trip 'em ;
And as for the loud Carolinian crowd,
Rhode Island alone, sir, can whip 'em !
Loyal and true little Rhody !
Bully for you, little Rhody !
Governor Sprague is a very good egg,
And worthy to lead little Rhody !

THF LONDON "TIMES" ON AMERICAN AFFAIRS.

AIR—Villikins and his Dinah.

John Bull vos a-valkin' his parlor von day,
Ha-fixin' the vorld wery much his hown vay,
Ven igstrawnary news cum from hover the sea,
Habout the great country vot brags it is free.

Ri tu ri li ru li ra, ri tu ri li ra,
Ri tu ri li ru li ra, ri tu ri li ra,
Ri tu ri li ru li ra, ri tu ri li ra,
Ri tu ri li ru li ra, ri tu ri li ra.

Hand these vos the tidins this news it did tell,
That great Yankee Doodle vos going to--vell,
That he vos a-volloped by Jefferson D.,
Hand no longer " some punkins" vos likely to be.
Ri tu ri li, &c.

John Bull, slyly vinkin,' then said hunto he ;
" My dear *Times*, my hold covey, go pitch hinto he ;
Let us vollop great Doodle now ven 'e is down ;
Hif ve vollops him vell, ve vill ' do 'im up brown.'
Ri tu ri li, &c.

" His long-legged boots hat my 'ed 'e 'as 'urled,
I'd rather not see 'em a-trampin' the vorld ;
Hand I howe him a grudge for his conduct so wile,
In himportin' shillalahs from Erin's green hile.
Ri tu ri li, &c.

"I knows Jefferson D. is a rascally chap,
Who goes hin for cribbin' the Guvurnment pap ;
That Hexeter 'All may be down upon me,
But as Jeff. 'as the cotton, I'll cotton to he.

Ri tu ri li, &c.

So Bull he vent hin the blockade for to bust ;
The Christians they cried, and the sinners they cussed ;
There vos blowin', and blusterin', and mighty parade,
And hall to get ready to break the blockade.

Ri tu ri li, &c.

Ven hall hof a sudden it come in the 'ed
Hof a prudent hold covey, who up and 'e said ;
"Hit's bad to vant cotton, but worser by far,
His the sufferin hand misery you'll make by a war.

Ri tu ri li, &c.

So he sent not 'is vessel hacross the broad sea,
Vich vos hawful 'ard lines for poor Jefferson D..
Hand wrote hunto Doodle, "'Old hon, and be true!"
And Jonathan hanswered Bull, "Bully for you!"

Ri tu ri li, &c.

SEQUEL AFTER-TIMES.

Has Bull vos valking in London haround,
'E found the *Times* lyin' hupon the cold ground,
With a big bale hof cotton right hover 'is side ;
Says Bull' "Hi perceive 'twas by cotton he died!"

———

THE BUGLE NOTE.

Air—Marseillaise.

Oh, freemen's sons arouse to battle,
'Gainst the proud, insulting foe ;
Shall their cannon 'round us rattle,
And no arm to strike a blow ?—
And no arm to strike a blow ?

Too long has tolerance been given,
 By forbearance kind and free ;
 But let now the war-cry be,
Our blest land shall ne'er be riven !
  To arms ! to arms, ye brave !
  Our trampled flag reclaim
From traitor's grasp, and nobly win
 A patriot's honored name.

Hear, hear the cannon loudly roaring,
 'Round our brave and valiant band ;
And a nation loud deploring
 The stained honor of our land—
 The stained honor of our land.
And will you tamely now surrender
 To a false and perjured host,
 Your glorious country's boast,
Refusing to defend her ?
  To arms ! to arms, ye brave !
  Our trampled flag reclaim
From traitor's grasp, and nobly win
 A patriot's honored name.

THE SOLDIER'S HYMN.

AIR—Old Hundred.

God of our fathers, on the earth,
 Girt for the fight, Thy servants stand ;
Oh, bless us, ere the trumpet sound,
 With strength from Thy almighty hand.

The cloud of war comes from the South ;
 The battle-storm bursts o'er our heads
Our starry flag a rainbow bright,
 A glory round our pathway sheds.

Our fathers' spirits watch that flag,
 They left to us without a stain ;
We take their motto in our hearts—
 " To die for Liberty is gain."

And when victorious we return,
 Oh, may those folds be pure and free,
As when our father, Washington,
 Gave us our Flag and Liberty.

Thou God of Battles, hear our prayer!
 From Western plains to Eastern coasts,
Strong in Thy blessing forth we march—
 Our trust is in the Lord of Hosts.

OUR FATHERLAND.

God save our Fatherland! from shore to shore;
God save our Fatherland, one evermore.
 No hand shall peril it,
 No strife shall sever it,
 East, West, and North and South!
 One evermore!
CHORUS—God save our Fatherland! true home of Free-
 dom!
God save our Fatherland, one evermore;
One in her hills and streams,
One in her glorious dreams,
One in Love's noblest themes—
 One evermore!

Strong in the hearts of men, love is thy throne;
Union and Liberty crown thee alone;
 Nations have sighed for thee;
 Our sires have died for thee;
 We'll all be true to thee—
 All are thine own.
 God save our Fatherland, &c.

Ride on, proud Ship of State, though tempests
 lower;
Ride on in majesty, glorious in power;
 Though fierce the blast may be,
 No wreck shall shatter thee—
 Storms shall but bring to thee
 Sunshine once more.
 God save our Fatherland, &c.

THE STRIPES AND THE STARS.

BY EDNA DEAN PROCTOR.

Air—The Star Spangled Banner.

Oh! Star Spangled Banner! the Flag of our pride!
Though trampled by traitors and basely defied,
Fling out to the glad winds your Red, White, and
 Blue,
For the heart of the North-land is beating for you!
And her strong arm is nerving to strike with a will
Till the foe and his boastings are humbled and still!
Here's welcome to wounding and combat and scars
And the glory of death--for the Stripes and the Stars!

From prairie, O ploughman! speed boldly away—
There's seed to be sown in God's furrows to-day—
Row landward, lone fisher! stout woodman come
 home!
Let smith leave his anvil and weaver his loom,
And hamlet and city ring loud with the cry,
" For God and our country we'll fight till we die!
Here's welcome to wounding and combat and scars
And the glory of death—for the Stripes and the Stars!"

Invincible Banner! the Flag of the Free!
Oh! where treads the foot that would falter for thee?
Or the hands to be folded, till triumph is won
And the Eagle looks proud, as of old, to the sun?
Give tears for the parting—a murmur of prayer—
Then Forward! the fame of our standard to share!
With welcome to wounding and combat and scars
And the glory of death—for the Stripes and the Stars.

O God of our Fathers! this Banner must shine
Where battle is hottest, in warfare divine!
The cannon has thundered, the bugle has blown—
We fear not the summons—we fight not alone!
Oh! lead us, till wide from the Gulf to the Sea
The land shall be sacred to Freedom and Thee!
With love, for oppression ; with blessing, for scars,—
One Country—one Banner--the Stripes and the Stars!

THE YANKEE VOLUNTEERS.

As sung by Private Ephraim Peabody, on the night after the march through Baltimore.

AIR—'Tis my delight on a shiny night.

Come, all ye true Americans that love the Stripes and
    Stars,
For which your gallant countrymen go marching to the
    wars ;
For grand old Massachusetts raise up three rousing
    cheers ;
Three times three and a ti-ger for the Yankee Volun-
    teers !

The nineteenth day of April they marched unto the
    war,
And on that day, upon the way, they stopped at Balti-
    more,
And trustingly expected the customary cheers
Which every loyal city gives the YankeeVolunteers.

But suddenly in fury there came a mighty crowd,
Led on by negro drivers, with curses long and loud,
With frenzied imprecations, with savage threats and
    sneers,
They welcomed to the city the Yankee Volunteers.

So furious grew the multitude, they rushed at them
    amain,
And a great storm of missiles came pouring like a rain.
Amid a thunderous clamor, such as mortal seldom
    hears,
They tried to cross the city, did the Yankee Volun-
    teers.

The murderous storm of missiles laid many a soldier
    low,
Yet still these gallant hearts forebore to give the an-
    swering blow,
Till all the miscreants shouted, "They're nearly dead
    with fears ;
We'll hurry up and finish these Yankee Volunteers."

But, lo ! the guns are leveled, and loud the volleys
  roar,
And, inch by inch, they fight their way through the
  streets of Baltimore ;
Before them shrunk the traitors, above them rise the
  cheers,
As through the throng, a myriad strong, march on the
  Volunteers.

Hurrah, then, for the old Bay State that stood so well
  at bay !
Hurrah, for those who shed their blood, and gave their
  lives away !
For grand old Massachusetts, boys, let's give three
  rousing cheers !
Three times three and a ti-ger for the Yankee Volunteers !

GOD SAVE OUR NATIVE LAND

BY JAMES WALDEN.

AIR—America.

God save our native land
From the invader's hand—
  Home of the free !
Though ruthless traitors aim
To crush our nation's fame,
Yet still, in Freedom's name,
  We cling to thee !

O Lord ! we humbly pray,
Far distant be the day
  Ere that shall be ;
Though lawless bands combine
To shatter Freedom's shrine,
With faith and hope divine
  We cling to thee !

O Lord ! when, hand to hand,
Brothers as foes shall stand,
  Shield Thou the right !

Stay these unhappy wars,
Join us in one great cause—
To guard our nation's laws
    With freemen's might!

Lord! may this strife soon cease;
Grant us a lasting peace—
    Parted we fall!
Long may our banner wave
Over the free and brave—
O Lord! our country save—
    God save us all!

A GOOD TIME COMING.

There is a good time coming, boys,
    A good time coming;
There's a good time coming, boys,
    Wait a little longer;
We may not live to see the day,
    But earth shall glisten in the ray
    Of the good time coming.
Cannon-balls may aid the truth,
    But thought's a weapon stronger;
We'll win our battles by its aid,
    Wait a little longer.
There's a good time coming, boys,
    A good time coming,
There's a good time coming, boys,
    Wait a little longer.

There's a good time coming, boys,
    A good time coming;
There's a good time coming, boys,
    Wait a little longer;
The pen shall supersede the sword,
And right, not might, shall be the lord,
    In the good time coming;
Worth, not birth, shall rule mankind,
    And be acknowledged stronger;
The proper impulse has been given,
    Wait a little longer.

There's a good time coming, boys,
   A good time coming,
There's a good time coming, boys,
   Wait a little longer.

A BIG THING ON ICE.

AIR—A good time coming, boys.

There's a big thing coming, boys,
   "A big thing on ice;"
There's a big thing coming, boys,
   Wait a little longer.
When we get ready to advance,
Oh! then we'll make Jeff. Davis dance,
   With the big thing coming;
Shinplasters may be plenty South,
   But gold and silver's stronger,
And we've strong arms to win the fight,
   Wait a little longer.
There's a big thing coming, boys,
   A big thing coming;
There's a big thing coming, boys,
   Wait a little longer.

There's a big thing coming, boys,
   A big thing coming;
There's a big thing coming, boys,
   Wait a little longer.
Treason and traitors we'll strike down,
Victory will all our efforts crown,
   With the big thing coming.
Could we but see McClellan's plan,
   It would not make us stronger,
Be steady, then, each Union man,
   And wait a little longer.
There's a big thing coming, boys,
   Wait a little longer;
There's a big thing coming, boys,
   Wait a little longer.

THE BRAVE BOYS OF COMPANY D.

Composed and respectfully dedicated to the officers and mem
bers of Company D, Tenth Regiment National Zouaves.

BY J. C. GOBRIGHT.

AIR—Rosin the Beau.

Come gather around, gallant soldiers,
    With hearts full of mirth and of glee ;
Joyfully join in the chorus,
    With the brave sons of Company D.

In the morning when reveille is over,
    Our hands then we joyfully rub,
Refreshed we arise from our clover,
And quickly fall in for our grub.

For guard and for drill always ready
    We attend to our earliest call,
And with steps that are firm and are steady,
    Fall into the ranks one and all.

At night when our duties are over,
    And all thought of our labor is fled,
We quickly spread out our cover,
    And nimbly jump into the bed.

When forward we march on the rebels,
    They will be in a terrible fix,
They will think that the devil is coming
    When they see Col. John E. Bendix.

Secession may boast of her cotton,
    But we will wind up some thread on her spool,
For by them it will not be forgotten,
    That we have the right sort of *Wool*,

To-night let us think of the loved ones,
    Who silently miss us at home ;
They know that we love and respect them,
    Although we have left them alone.

To our parents, our sisters, our brothers,
　Our wives and our children so dear,
Our sweethearts, our friends, and all others,
　Let us fill up and drink them good cheer.

Let us sing and now wind up the chorus,
　And think of the work we have to do ;
We have plenty of fighting before us,
　If we stand by " the Red, White, and Blue!"

THE DIXIE OF OUR UNION.

Let all good Union men about
Come join us in a glorious shout,
　Hurrah! hurrah! hurrah! hurrah!
For Union and our Country dear,
We'll raise aloft a hearty cheer,
　Hurrrh! hurrah! hurrah! hurrah!

CHORUS.—Then for our Union we will stand,
　　　　Hurrah! hurrah!
　　　And all, throughout this happy land,
　　　Will join together heart and hand;
Hurrah! hurrah! Then hurrah for our Union!
Hurrah! hurrah! Then hurrah for our Union!

Let us unite with all our might,
And drive Disunion from our sight,
　Hurrah! &c.
And let all people know their doom,
If they too much on us presume ;
　Hurrah! &c.
　　　Then for our Union, &c.

Oh! may our Stars and Stripes still wave
Forever o'er the Free and Brave !
　Hurrah! &c.
And let our motto ever be—
For Union and for Liberty !
　Hurrah! &c.
　　　Then for our Union, &c.

From Maine to Texas let the cry
Of Union mount up to the sky,
   Hurrah ! &c.
And from Atlantic may its roar
Be heard on old Pacific's shore;
   Hurrah ! &c.
      Then for our Union, &c.

And now, dear friends, let one and all,
Respond unto his Country's call,
   Hurrah ! &c.
For Union in our land so blest,
From North to South, from East to West,
   Hurrah ! &c.
      Then for our Union, &c.

A YANKEE SHIP AND A YANKEE CREW.

A Yankee ship and a Yankee crew,
   Tally hi ho ! you know !
O'er the bright blue waves like a sea-bird flew,
   Singing hey ! aloft and alow !
Her sails are spread to the fairy breeze,
  The spray sparkling as thrown from her prow,
Her flag is the proudest that floats on the seas,
  When homeward she's steering now.
     A Yankee ship, &c.

A Yankee ship and a Yankee crew,
   Tally hi ho ! you know ! ·
With hearts aboard both gallant and true,
   The same aloft and alow.
The blackened sky and the whistling wind
  Foretell the approach of a gale,
And home and its joys flit over each mind ;
  Husbands, lovers, on deck there ! a sail !
Distress is the word, God speed them through—
   Bear a hand aloft and alow !
     A Yankee ship, &c.

A Yankee ship and a Yankee crew,
    Tally hi ho ! you know !
Freedom defends the land where it grew—
    We're free aloft and alow !
Bearing down is a ship in regal pride,
    Defiance at each mast-head ;
She's wrecked, and the one bears that floats alongside
    The Stars and the Stripes, still to victory wed,
That ne'er strike to a foe while the sky is blue,
    Or a tar's aloft and alow.
        A Yankee ship, &c.

"DIXIE," OF THE MICHIGAN BOYS.

Away down South where grows the cotton,
'Seventy-six seems quite forgotten ;
Far away, far away, far away, Dixie land.
And men with rebel shout and thunder
Tear our good old flag asunder ;
Far away, far away, far away, Dixie land.

CHORUS.—Then we're bound for the land of Dixie,
    Hurrah ! hurrah !
In Dixie land we'll take our stand,
And plant our flag in Dixie, away, away,
Away down South in Dixie, away, away,
Away down South in Dixie.

That flag—the foeman quailed before it,
When our patriot fathers bore it ;
Far away, far away, far away, Dixie land.
And battle fields are shrined in story,
Where its folds were bathed in glory ;
Far away, far away, far away, Dixie land.
    Then we're bound, &c.

And now when traitor hands assail it,
Staunch defenders ne'er shall fail it ;
Far away, far away, far away, Dixie land.

Nor from its glorious constellation
Stars be plucked by pirate nation ;
Far away, far away, far away, Dixie land.
　　Then we're bound, &c.

Undimmed shall float that starry banner,
Over Charleston and Savannah ;
Far away, far away, far away, Dixie land.
And Bunker Hill and Pensacola
Own alike its mission holy ;
Far away, far away, far away, Dixie land.
　　Then we're bound, &c.

Yes, sound the march !　Our Northern freemen
Turn not back for man or demon,
Far away, far away, far away, Dixie land.
Until once more our banner glorious
Waves o'er Dixie land victorious,
Far away, far away, far away, Dixie land.
　　Then we'll plant our flag in Dixie !
　　　　Hurrah ! hurrah !
Whoever hauls the old flag down,
　　We'll shoot him down in Dixie !
Away, away, away down South in Dixie !
Away, away, away down South in Dixie !

O'TOOLE AND McFINNIGAN ON THE WAR.

Air—Barnaby Finegan.

Two Irishmen out of employ,
　And out at the elbows as aiz'ly,
Adrift in a grocery store,
　Were smoking and taking it lazily.
The one was a broth of a boy,
　Whose cheek-bones turned out and turned in
　　again,
His name it was Paddy O'Toole,
　The other was Misther McFinnigan.

"I think of enlistin'," says Pat,
    "Because, do ye see what o'clock it is?
There's nothin' adoin' at all,
    But drinking at Mrs. O'Docharty's.
It's not until after the war
    That business times will begin again,
And fightin's the duty of all"—
    "You're right, sir," says Misther McFinnigan.

'Bad luck to the rebels, I say,
    For kickin' up all of this bobbery,
They call themselves gintlemin, too,
    While practisin' murder and robbery;
Now, if it's gintale for to stale,
    And take all your creditors in again,
I'm glad I'm no gintleman born"—
    "You're right, sir," says Misther McFinnigan.

"The spalpeens make bould to remark,
    Their chivalry couldn't be ruled by us;
And, by the same token, I think
    They're never too smart to be fooled by us.
Now, if it's the nagurs they mane
    Be chivalry, then it's a sin again
To fight for a cause that is black"—
    "You're right, sir," says Misther McFinnigan.

"Och, hone! but it's hard that a swate
    Good-lookin' young chap like myself, indade,
Should loose his ten shillin's a day,
    Because of the throuble the South has made;
But that's just the reason, ye see,
    Why I should help Union to win again,
It's that will bring wages once more"—
    "You're right, sir," says Misther McFinnigan.

"Joost mind what old England's about,
    A sending her throops into Canaday,
And all her ould ships on the coast
    Are ripe for some treachery any day;

Now if she should mix in the war—
 Be jabers ! it makes me head spin again—
Ould Ireland would have such a chance !"—
"You're right, sir," says Misther McFinnigan.

"Och, murther ! me blood's in a blaze,
 To think of bould Corcoran leading us
Right into the camp of the bastes
 Whose leeches so long have been bleeding us!
The Stars and the Stripes here at home,
 To Canada walls we would pin again,
And wouldn't we raise them in Cork ?"
"You're right, sir," says Misther McFinnigan.

"And down at the South, do ye mind,
 There's plinty of Irishmen mustering,
Deluded to fight for the wrong
 By rebel mis-statements and blustering ;
But once let ould England, their foe,
 To fight for the Union begin again,
And sure, they'd desert to a man !"
"You're right, sir," says Misther McFinnigan.

"Hurroo ! for the Union, me boys,
 And divil take all who would bother it ;
Secession's a nagur so black
 The divil himself ought to father it !
Hurroo for the bould 69th,
 That's prisintly bound to go in again ;
It's Corcoran's rescue they're at"—
"You're right, sir," says Misther McFinnigan.

"I'm off right away to enlist,
 And sure won't the bounty be handy-O !
To kape me respectably dressed,
 And furnish me dudheens and brandy-O !
I'm thinkin', me excellent friend,
 You're eyeing that bottle of gin again ;
You wouldn't mind thryin' a dhrop"—
"You're *right*, sir," says Misther McFinnigan.

COME, LANDLORDS, FILL,

CHORUS—Come, landlords, fill your flowing bowl,
  Until it doth run over ;
  For to-night we'll merry, merry be,
  To-morrow we'll get sober.

SOLO—The man that drinks good whiskey-punch,
  And goes to bed mellow,
  Lives as he ought to live,
  And dies a clever fellow.

    Come, landlords, &c.

  The man that drinks cold water, boys,
  And goes to bed sober,
  Falls as the leaves do fall,
  And dies in October.

    Come, landlords, &c.

  But he who drinks just what he wants,
  And getteth half seas over,
  Will live until he dies, perhaps,
  And then lie down in clover.

    Come, landlords, &c.

THE STAR SPANGLED BANNER.

Oh ! say, can you see, by the dawn's early light,
  What so proudly we hailed at the twilight's last
    gleaming ?
Whose stripes and bright stars, through the perilous fight,
  O'er the ramparts we watched, were so gallantly
    streaming ;
And the rocket's red glare, the bombs bursting in air,
Gave proof through the night that our flag was still
    there.
CHORUS.—Oh ! say, does that star-spangled banner yet
    wave
      O'er the land of the free and the home of the
        brave ?

On the shore, dimly seen through the mist of the deep,
  Where the foe's haughty host in dread silence reposes,
What is that which the breeze, o'er the towering steep,
  As it fitfully blows, half conceals, half discloses?
Now it catches the gleam of the morning's first beam;
In full glory reflected, now shines in the stream.
  'Tis the the star-spangled banner—Oh! long may it
    wave
  O'er the land of the free, and the home of the brave!

And where is that band who so vauntingly swore,
  'Mid the havoc of war, and the battle's confusion,
A home and a country they'd leave us no more?
  Their blood has washed out their foul footstep's polu-
    tion;
No refuge could save the hireling and slave
From the terror of flight, or the gloom of the grave.
  And the star-spangled banner in triumph doth wave
  O'er the land of the free and the home of the brave!

Oh! thus be it ever, when freemen shall stand
  Between their loved home and war's desolation!
Blessed with victory and peace, may the heaven-rescued
    land
  Praise the power that has made and preserved us
    a nation;
Then conquer we must, when our cause it is just,
And this be our motto: "In God is our trust!"
  And the star-spangled banner in triumph shall wave
  O'er the land of the free and the home of the brave!

ADDITIONAL VERSE, BY OLIVER WENDELL HOLMES.

When our land is illumined by Liberty's smile,
  If a foe from within strike a blow at her glory,
Down, down with the traitor that dares to defile
  The flag of her stars and the page of her story!
By the millions unchained when our birthright was
    gained,
We will keep her bright blazon forever unstained!
  And the star-spangled banner in triumph shall wave
  While the land of the free is the home of the brave!

ADDITIONAL VERSE, BY MISS STEBBINS, THE SCULPTOR.

When treason's dark cloud hovers black o'er the land,
    And traitors conspire to sully her glory,
When that banner is torn by a fratricide band,
    Whose bright, starry folds shine illumined in story,
United we stand for the dear native land,
To the Union we pledge every heart, every hand !
    And the star-spangled banner in triumph shall wave
O'er the land of the free and the home of the brave!

COME, RAISE THE BANNER HIGH.

BY FRANCIS B. MURTHA.

Air—'Tis my delight on a shiny night.

Come, raise that banner high, my boys,
    Hang out the Stripes and Stars ;
Forever wave that glorious flag
    Above the Stars and Bars.
Where'er it floats in freedom's cause
    All discord disappears ;
For it's our delight to march and fight
    As Union Volunteers.

Then shout, shout, shout the loud huzza,
    And pledge each heart and hand
To fight the Union's glorious cause—
    Drive treason from the land ;
To make those Southern rebels crave
    Our pardon with their tears ;
For it's our delight to march and fight
    As Union Volunteers.

McClellan leads the army, boys !
    Our country's hope and pride !
Already cries of victory
    Redound on every side !
Then shout the war-cry loud, my boys,
    Banish coward fears ;
For it's our delight to march and fight
    As Union Volunteers.

A GLASS IS GOOD.

A glass is good, and a lass is good,
    And a pipe is good in cold weather ;
The world is good, and the people are good,
    And we're all good fellows together.
A bottle is a very good thing,
    With a good deal of good wine in it ;
A song is good, when a body can sing,
    And to finish, we must begin it.

CHORUS.—For a glass is good, and a lass is good,
        And a pipe is good in cold weather ;
        The world is good, and the people are good,
        And we're all good fellows together.

A friend is good when you're out of good luck,
    For that is the time to try him ;
For a Justice, good the haunch of a buck—
    With such a good present you'll buy him.
A fine old woman is good, when she's dead ;
    A rogue very good for good hanging ;
A fool is good by the nose to be led,
    And my song deserves a good banging.
        For a glass is good, &c.

CORPORAL KELLY.

AIR—Barnaby Finegan.

Away with the mallet and chisel—
    No more of a stone-cutter's life ;
My books and my papers shall mizzle,
    For I'll follow the drum and the fife.
I was once a stone-cutter, hard-fisted,
    But the "ranks" had a charm for my eye ;
So I bent down my head, and I 'listed
    To the tune of the "Bould Soger Boy."

I am covered with trappings and facings,
    And a gilt eagle sits on my cap ;
I am learning my marchings and facings,
    And at last I'm a good-looking chap.

Oh ! bomb-shells may fly like the divil —
 They may blow up foundation and roof--
They can light on my head ; and be civil,
 For, d'ye mind, it's intirely bomb-proof.

I've courage enough, I am thinking,
 And I'll always the enemy meet ;
But when a friend's glass I am drinking,
 I'll not be the last at re-treat.
The ladies can't help but desire me,
 Since I've caught their sweet hearts in a trap ;
But there's one that must never admire me—
 Her name, I believe, is "Miss Hap."

The whip never marked my broad back,
 Nor gave my big stomach the gripes ;
Yet I may be stretched on the rack,
 If I haven't been getting the stripes.
But the stripes, you must know, were no harm—
 They were a great honor, I tell ye ;
For they were all laid on my arm,
 And I am bould Corporal Kelly.

AULD LANG SYNE.

Should auld acquaintance be forgot,
 And never brought to mind,
Should auld acquaintance be forgot,
 And days o' lang syne.
CHORUS—For auld lang syne, my dear,
 For auld lang syne,
 We'll tak' a cup o' kindness yet,
 For auld lang syne.

We twa ha'e run about the braes,
 And pu'd the gawans fine ;
But we've wandered many a weary foot
 Sin auld lang syne.
  For auld lang syne, &c.

We twa ha'e paid let i' the burn,
  Frae morning sun till dine ;
But seas between us braid ha'e roared,
  Sin auld lang syne.

> For auld lang syne, &c.

And there's a hand, my trusty feire,
  And gie's a hand'o' thine ;
And we'll tak' a right gude willie waught
  For auld lang syne.

> For auld lang syne, &c.

And surely you'll be your pint stoup,
  And surely I'll be mine ;
And we'll tak' a cup o' kindness yet,
  For auld lang syne.

> For auld lang syne, &c.

DRINK IT DOWN.

A popular Camp Song.

Here's success to Port,
Chorus — Drink it down, drink it down,
Here's success to Port,
Chorus.—Drink it down.
Here's success to Port,
For it warms the heart for sport,
Drink it down, drink it down, drink it down.

Here's success to Sherry,
    Drink it down, drink it down,
Here's success to Sherry,
    Drink it down.
Here's success to Sherry,
    For it makes the heart beat merry,
Drink it down, drink it down, drink it down.

Here's success to Whiskey,
    Drink it down, drink it down,
Here's success to Whiskey,
    Drink it down.
Here's success to Whiskey,
For it makes the spirits frisky,
Drink it down, drink it down, drink it down.

Here's success to cider,
    Drink it down, drink it down,
Here's success to cider,
    Drink it down.
Here's success to cider,
For it makes the frame grow wider,
Drink it down, drink it down, drink it down.

Here's success to Brandy,
    Drink it down, drink it down,
Here's success to Brandy,
    Drink it down.
Here's success to Brandy,
Just enough to make us handy,
Drink it down, drink it down, drink it down.

Here's success to Ale,
    Drink it down, drink it down,
Here's success to Ale,
    Drink it down.
Here's success to Ale,
When its made us strong and hale,
Drink it down, drink it down, drink it down.

Here's success to Punch,
    Drink it down, drink it down,
Here's success to Punch,
    Drink it down.
Here's success to Punch,
With a little social lunch,
Drink it down, drink it down, drink it down.

Here's success to Porter,
 Drink it down, drink it down,
Here's success to Porter,
 Drink it down.
Here's success to Porter,
While we use it as we " oughter,"
Drink it down, drink it down, drink it down.

Here's success to Water,
 Drink it down, drink it down,
Here's success to Water,
 Drink it down.
Here's success to Water,
Heaven's draught that does no slaughter,
Drink it down, drink it down, drink it down.

AMERICA.

My country, 'tis of thee,
Sweet land of Liberty,
 Of thee I sing :
Land where my fathers died,
Land of the Pilgrims' pride,
From every mountain-side,
 Let freedom ring.

My native country, thee,
Land of the noble, free—
 Thy name I love :
I love the rocks and rills,
Thy woods and templed hills ;
My heart with rapture thrills
 Like that above.

Let music swell the breeze,
And ring from all the trees
 Sweet freedom's song :
Let mortal tongues awake,
Let all that breathes partake,
Let rocks their silence break,
 The sound prolong.

Our fathers' God, to thee,
Author of liberty,
    To thee I sing :
Long may our land be bright
With freedom's holy light ;
Protect us by thy might,
    Great God our King.

UNION AND JUSTICE.

AIR—Flag of our Union.

For Union and Victory with firmness we stand ;
    For Union and Justice victorious ;
The Union of Right and the Hope of our land,
    Whose brow wears the crown ever glorious.
Our banners are waving o'er every State
    Where Liberty's lovers are dwelling,
And the voices of cannonry, orators great,
    Of the glory of Union, are telling.
CHORUS—For Union and Justice victorious, victorious ;
        For Union and Justice victorious, victorious ;
            United we fight
            The battle of Right,
    For Union and Justice victorious.

Our motto is " Right," and such ever shall be ;
    Our battle-cry, " Union forever ;"
Our souls, true to Justice, shall ever be free,
    And shall bow down to Severance never.
American hearts, patriotic and strong,
    American hearts charged with bravery,
For Union and Justice now wrestle with Wrong,
    In the war between Honor and Knavery.

        For Union and Justice, &c.

Oh ! men of Columbia, be loyal and true !
    Be firm in the midst of the battle,
And never, ne'er shrink while there's something to do,
    Tho' the enemy's shot 'round you rattle !

If strong in our strength as our hope we will be,
  And as true as our object is glorious,
We'll add a new star to the flag of the free,
  And make Union and Justice victorious.
     For Union and Justice, &c.

SONGS OF THE CAMP.

BY BAYARD TAYLOR.

Air—The girls we left behind us.

" Give us a song !" the soldiers cried,
  The outer trenches guarding,
When the heated gun of the camp allied
  Grew weary of bombarding.

The dark Redan, in silent scoff,
  Lay, grim and threatening, under,
And the tawny mouth of the Malakoff
  No longer belched its thunder.

There was a pause. The guardman said
" We storm the forts to-morrow ;
Sing while we may, another day
  Will bring enough of sorrow."

They lay along the battery's side,
  Below the smoking cannon—
Brave hearts from Severn and from Clyde,
  And from the banks of Shannon.

They sang of love and not of fame—
  Forgot was Britain's glory .
Each heart recalled a different name,
  But all sang—" Annie Laurie."

Voice after voice caught up the song,
  Until its tender passion
Rose like an anthem, rich and strong—
  Their battle eve confession.

Dear girl—her name he dared not speak—
Yet, as the song grew louder,
Something upon the soldier's cheek
Washed off the stains of powder.

Beyond the darkening ocean burned
The bloody sunsets embers,
While the Crimean valleys learned
How English love remembers.

And Irish Nora's eyes are dim,
For a singer, dumb and gory !
And English Mary mourns for him
Who sang of '' Annie Laurie.''

Ah ! soldiers, to your honored rest
Your truth and valor bearing :
The bravest are the tenderest—
The loving are the daring !

THE GALLANT ZOUAVES.

Air—Nelly Bly.

Zouaves sly, shut one eye
When they go to sleep;
But where spies and traitors lurk,
One eye they open keep.

Hi, Zouaves ! ho, Zouaves ! don't be napping now,
But, day or night, just for a fight, be ready anyhow !

When they march they lift their feet,
And then they set them down ;
But when they *fight* there's music in
That part of the town !
Hi, Zouaves ! ho, Zouaves ! &c.

When they sing, their roaring voice
　So frightful is to hear,
That, at the sound, from all around,
　The rebels cut and clear!
　　　　Hi, Zouaves! ho, Zouaves! &c.

Beauregard is puffing hard
　To head off General Scott;
And Jeff he keeps his horse in reach
　To run before he's shot!
　　　　Hi, Zouaves! ho, Zouaves! &c.

The F. F.'s shirk the dirty work---
　Before the fight begins
They set a row of niggers up
　To save their own poor skins.
　　　　Hi, Zouaves! ho, Zouaves! &c.

Boys, hurrah! we'll teach the law
　To Letcher and to Wise;
Hemp and pine-wood for each scamp
　‘Who our flag defies.
Hi, Zouaves! ho, Zouaves! three cheers for your cause!
Your arms keep bright, your hearts keep light—brave
　guardians of the laws!

PAT'S OPINION OF THE STARS AND STRIPES.

BY JOHN F. POOLE.

Sung, with great applause, by Fred May.
Air—Darling Ould Stick.

I've got a new song for to sing ye's to night,
It's intended to put the Blue Devils to flight;
That it's got a fine chorus to you will be shown,
And the man that wont sing it can let it alone.
　　It's of the blackguards our country that's ruinin';
　　The traitors all houlding communion;
　　A trying to bust up the Union
　　　And pull *down* the Stars and the Stripes.

Whin the rebils first hoisted their flag of seven Stars,
With the bould Sixty-ninth I wint off to the wars ;
Tho' the foes they were thick and our numbers but few,
Faix, we made a charge on a masked battery or two.
    Though we'd bate five to one on the livel,
    With a foe that would only act civil ;
    Now. I tell ye's we fought like the divil,
        Uphoulding the Stars and the Stripes.

Then the bold Fire Zouaves—'twas delightful to see
How they cut up the famous Black Horse cavalry ;
And the foe got a taste, too, of ould Bunker Hill,
For the brave Massachusetts boys fought with a will.
    They wint in with a whoop and a shout, sirs !
    For the *Union !* it was their cry out, sirs!
    Oh! the rebils found they were about, sirs,
        Upholding the Stars and the Stripes.

Then at Port Royal, too, was the divil to pay,
When they found Uncle Sam had his fleet on the say,
And was coming to bate them like rats in a pit,
And to show them no marcy, bad luck to the bit.
    For while they were trembling with fear, sirs,
    Their flag tumbled down 'bout their ears, sirs,
    While up went, with three hearty cheers, sirs,
        The beautiful Stars and the Stripes.

We'll soon bate the blackguards afloat and ashore,
And our flag o'er *Fort Sumter* be waving once more ;
Now they'd better give in, for we'll soon gain the day,
And *Corcoran*, too, we'll have back in the fray.
    Whin the Star-Spangled banner he raises ;
    Sure, he'll capture ould Jefferson Davis ;
    And will wallop the rebels like blazes,
        An' will die with the *Stars* and the *Stripes !*

HAIL COLUMBIA.

Hail, Columbia, happy land ! hail, ye heroes, heaven-
    born band.
    Who fought and bled in Freedom's cause,
    Who fought and bled in Freedom's cause,

And when the storm of war was gone, enjoyed the peace
    your valor won.
Let independence be our boast, ever mindful what it cost ;
Ever grateful for the prize, let its altar reach the skies.

CHORUS—Firm, united, let us be, rallying round our lib-
       erty ;
         As a band of brothers joined, peace and safety
         we shall find.

Immortal patriots, rise once more, defend your rights,
    defend your shore.
Let no rude foe, with impious hand,
Let no rude foe, with impious hand,
Invade the shrine where sacred lies, of toil and blood,
    the well-earned prize.
While offering peace sincere and just, in heaven we place
    a manly trust
That truth and justice will prevail, and every shame of
    bondage fail.

Sound, sound the trump of fame ! let Washington's
    great name
Ring through the world with loud applause,
Ring through the world with loud applause,
Let every clime to Freedom dear, listen with a joyful ear.
With equal skill and God-like power, he govern'd in the
    fearful hour
Of horrid war ! or guides, with ease, the happier times
    of honest peace.

Behold the chief who now commands, again to serve his
    country stands—
The rock on which the storm will beat,
The rock on which the storm will beat,
But armed in virtue firm and true, his hopes are fixed on
    Heaven and you.
When hope was sinking in dismay, and gloom obscured
    Columbia's day,
His steady mind, from changes free, resolved on death
    or liberty.

LET COWARDS SHIRK THEIR DUTY.

AIR—The Low-Backed Car.

Let cowards shirk their duty,
    And falter from the fray ;
My post I'll find, nor shrink behind,
    When honor calls away.
For Union and for Freedom,
    I'll wield a sword or gun,
And take my stand, for laws and land,
    Till the battle's nobly won.

CHORUS.—For I follow the Stripes and Stars,
        No matter for wounds or scars,
    And I'll act my part,
        With my arm and heart,
    In defence of the Stripes and Stars.

The truth is past denying,
    That danger's close at hand,
And I do love, all things above,
    My own dear native land.
So where the conflict rages,
    And where our foeman be,
To stand or fall, at Union's call,
    There is the place for me.
        For I follow, &c.

May God bless those who love me,
    And those I love defend ;
If life I give, to those who live
    My dear ones I commend.
But while the cannon's booming,
    And trumpets loudly blare,
The Union's cause, the land and laws,
    Must be my only care.
        For I follow, &c.

www.ingramcontent.com/pod-product-compliance
Lightning Source LLC
Chambersburg PA
CBHW030025030726
47499CB00008B/3117